A HOME IN THE BARN

By the author of *Goodnight Moon*
MARGARET WISE BROWN

Pictures by Caldecott Medalist
JERRY PINKNEY

HARPER

An Imprint of HarperCollinsPublishers

Here is the barn
Hear the wind rattle
Open the door
And see all the cattle.

Outside in the cold
Hear the wind rattle

Stay in the barn
Keep warm with the cattle.

SQUEAK
SQUEAK

The field mice came creeping out of a hole
from out of the field, where they had lived
all summer and all fall.

The time had come for them to move
out of their little grass nests in the field
and into the big warm barn.

NEIGH SHIVER
SHIVER

The breath of the horses rose like smoke
in the cold air. And the winter wind told
them it was time to move into the big
warm barn.

In the big warm barn all the animals
were waking up, slowly and hungrily,
except for the little mice in the hayloft,
who had been up all night and were
just going to bed.

High up in the rafters of the barn, the swallows began to chirp in their deep, warm nests of mud.

Just as the dawn broke,
the bats came whizzing home.

And the cat curled up
for a little snooze.

MOOOOOOOO

A cow had a calf.

"Winter Morn will be her name," said Jonathan, the farmer, as he rubbed down her silky little curly coat. "Lucky she was born in the barn and not in the open field."

BIFF BANG BANG

The proud bull, Sahari, was stomping in his stall. He had just been dreaming of another bull and was raring for a fight.

Here is the barn
Hear the wind rattle
Outside in the cold
The winter had come whistling in.

WHOOOO

The little fat pony who had been sleeping late jumped up in his stall and scared all the little calves in the barn.

NEIGH
HRUMPH
HRUMPH

And with so many animals
all close together in the barn,
it was quite warm.

Outside in the cold
Hear the wind rattle
Come to the barn
Keep warm with the cattle.

Here is the barn
Hear the wind rattle
Open the door
And see all the cattle.

ARTIST'S NOTE

When I was asked to consider illustrating *A Home in the Barn*, a text authored by Margaret Wise Brown, her legacy and grand contribution to our world of children's literature immediately came to mind. Brown was a talented artist who, with just a few words and a rhythmic pace, could bring her narratives to life. She teased our imaginations, making readers pay closer attention to the magical world around us. That's exactly what happened as I read *A Home in the Barn* the first time: this poetic verse about farm animals seeking shelter for the winter awakened my curiosity, and I began to see smaller things in a big way. A cow gives birth to a calf during the first snowfall, so in looking for inspiration to begin making the pictures, I thought of Edward Hicks's painting *The Peaceable Kingdom* and Grant Wood's *Haystack in the Snow* and Andrew Wyeth's *Young Bull*.

The relationships between the animals also reminded me of my great-granddaughter's two short-haired, black tabby cats, Catty and Precious, that I have often felt know each other's needs. But intriguingly, the animals aren't the only characters in this story. There are two supporting actors—the blustery wind and the barn itself—and I knew my challenge would be to make the wind visible and give a muted voice to the barn. I chose drifting leaves and slightly bent grasses, cornstalks, and trees to suggest the presence of the wind. For the barn, I decided on the color red, to speak to its essential role as a place of warmth and safety.

Jerry Pinkney

To artists whose works express the rhythm,
harmony, and boundless beauty of farm life
—J.P.

A Home in the Barn ♦ Text copyright © 2018 by Hollins University ♦ Illustrations copyright © 2018 Jerry Pinkney ♦ All rights reserved. Manufactured in China. ♦ No part of this book may be used or reproduced in any manner whatsoever without written permission except in the case of brief quotations embodied in critical articles and reviews. For information address HarperCollins Children's Books, a division of HarperCollins Publishers, 195 Broadway, New York, NY 10007. ♦ www.harpercollinschildrens.com ♦ Library of Congress Control Number: 2017954090 ♦ ISBN 978-0-06-623787-9 ♦ The artist used pencil, watercolors, gouache, and pastel to create the illustrations for this book. ♦ Typography by Jeanne Hogle
18 19 20 21 22 SCP 10 9 8 7 6 5 4 3 2 1 ♦ ❖ ♦ First Edition